the CRAZY world of LOVE

Cartoons by
Roland Fiddy

EXLEY

Published in Great Britain by Exley Publications Ltd.
16 Chalk Hill, Watford, Herts WD1 4BN, United Kingdom.
Second and third printing 1989
Fourth printing 1990

ISBN 1-85015-097-4

Printed and bound in Hungary.

"Oh, John, I've never met anyone like you before …
Oh, Mark, I've never met anyone like you before …
Oh, Steve, I've never met anyone like you before …"

"Susan was right – you __ARE__ homely!"

"Not _THOSE_ thoughts!"

"*I don't know her name ... Just write 'the beautiful girl at the bacon counter in our supermarket'.*"

"*I think I should warn you Dad's a bit Victorian!*"

"I'm not a good judge of men, so I always let Bruce decide who comes in for coffee!"

"If you're going to sit there and sulk, you might as well go home!"

"You'll never get married George – you live in a protected little world of your own!"

1.

2.

3.

4.

5.

"And you still have the wavy hair I fell for, George!"

"Don't laugh, but my mates had to explain to me exactly what a blind date was!"

"My, you really are scared of women, aren't you?"

"I hope that young tearaway hasn't been hanging around!"

"We'll have to stop meeting like this – I forget what you look like!"

"I never get tired of reading 'Wuthering Heights' –
it could be us!"

Irresistible

1.

2.

"Excuse me, Sir, but if you don't replace your tie I must ask you to leave!"

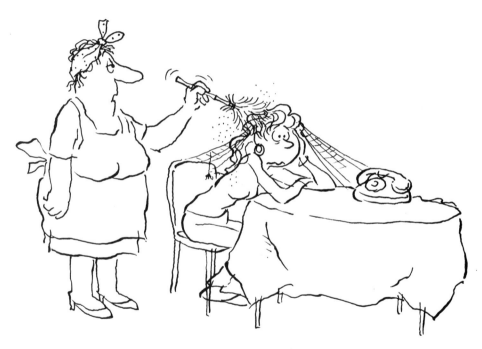

"*You might as well face it – he's stood you up!*"

"These are my parents – they are inseparable!"

"You're just testing me, aren't you Dorothy?"

"There's someone else, isn't there?"

"I'm not a bit tired, dear. It's only us old folks who have time to listen to your problems!"

"That's what I love about you, Lorna – you're such a good listener!"

"Our love has grown with the years!"

"When Mary left me I went to pieces – if I hadn't met you, Gloria, I think I'd have gone out of my mind!"

"Of course I'm not drunk Helen – wine never goes
to my head!"

"*Either we are witnesses to a unique astronomical phenomenon, Miss Johnson, or I'm in love!*"

BOY MEETS GIRL!

4. & 4a.

5. & 5a.

6. & 6a.

"Are you <u>sure</u> she's expecting you?"

"<u>Now</u> what's wrong?"

1.

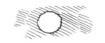

2.

3.

4.

5.

6.

7.

8.

"*Perhaps you would prefer to order later, Sir?*"

"Yes, Sigmund, I know you love and understand me
– I just can't take it any more!"

1.

2.

3.

4.

5.

6.

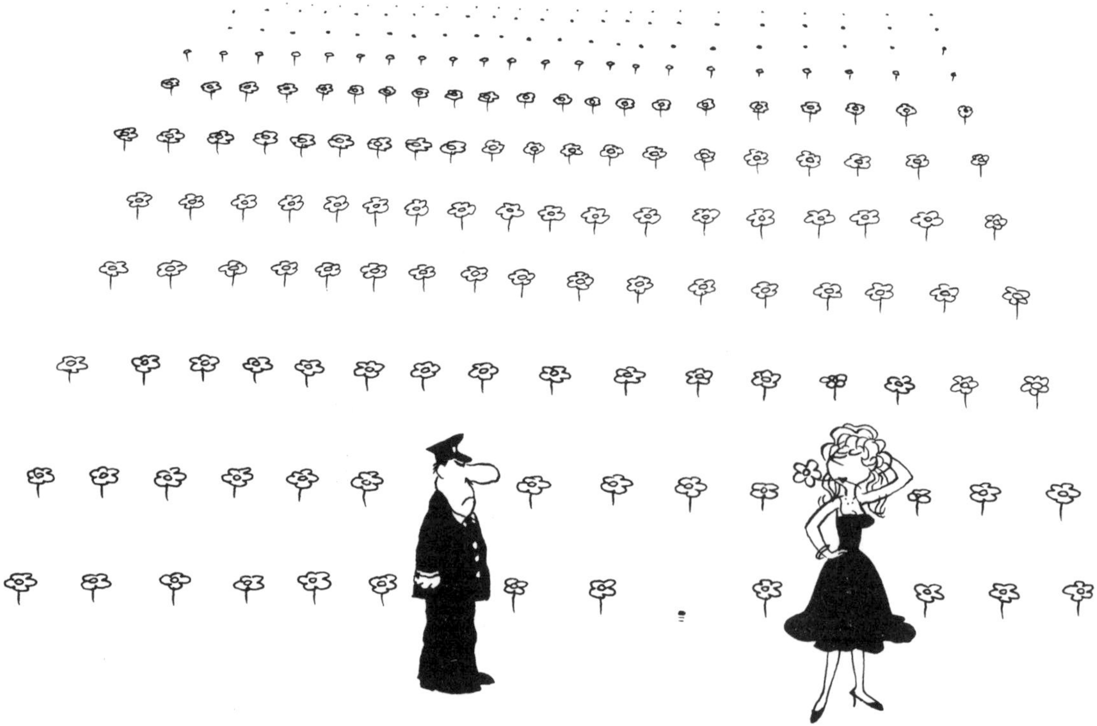

"When I was a boy, we had to entertain ourselves!"

"All these years we've been together Charlie, you've never changed!"

"When Lorna said she'd had a magical evening out with you, I didn't believe her."

"I told the tattooist to put 'mother' – unfortunately he was hard of hearing …"

1.

2.

6.

7.

8.

"But first, I have a suggestion …"

"Don't let a newspaper smother our great love!"

"I think I've found the right one for you – optimistic,
different, a wonderful sense of fun …

"Him? Just an old hanger-on!"

"John! No, I'm not doing anything – just sitting around."

"Alone at last!!"

"Dad's really taken to you!"

1.

2.

3.

"She won't be long – she's just shaving her legs."

"I take it you're going out with Linda this evening, son?"

"You <u>are</u> all things to all men, Sandra – that's the
trouble!"

"I think it makes you look distinguished!"

"I need more time, Henry!"

"The telephone is red hot again!"

"That's what I love about you Emily – you always laugh at my joke!"

"*On second thoughts, you look better with them on.*"

"I have a confession – under the feathers I'm bald!"

"Don't tell me – she's in love <u>again</u>!"

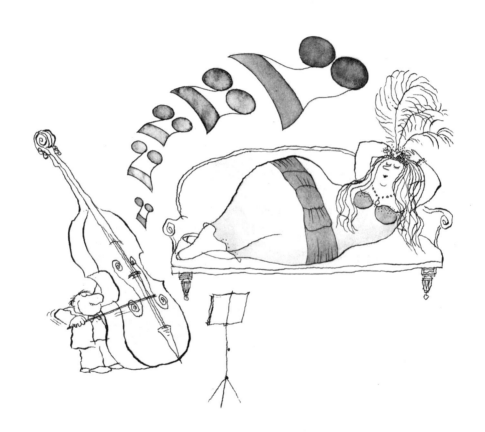

"*Macho men do not appeal to me, Bernard!*"

"We are in love with you, John Brown!"

"Sometimes I wish you would express your abiding love some other way!"

1.

2.

3.

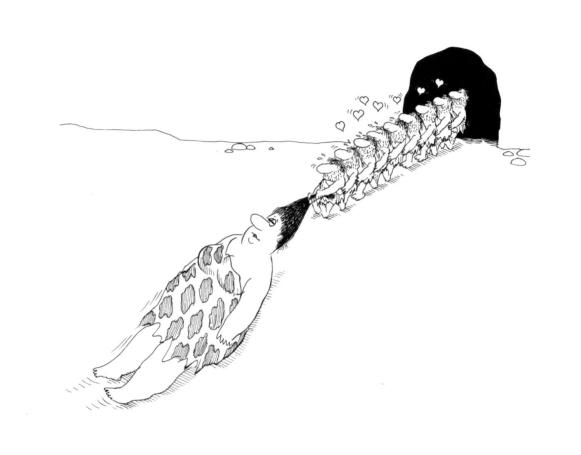

"Why don't you marry him and put us both out of our misery?"

Books in the "Crazy World" series:

The Crazy World of Birdwatching. £3.99. By Peter Rigby. Over eighty cartoons on the strange antics of the twitcher brigade. One of our most popular pastimes, this will be a natural gift for any birdwatcher.

The Crazy World of Cricket. £3.99. By Bill Stott. This must be Bil Stott's silliest cartoon collection. It makes an affectionate present for any cricketer who can laugh at himself.

The Crazy World of Gardening. £3.99. By Bill Stott. The perfect present for anyone who has ever wrestled with a lawnmower that won't start, over-watered a pot plant or been assaulted by a rose bush from behind.

The Crazy World of Golf. £3.99. By Mike Scott. Over eighty hilarious cartoons show the fanatic golfer in his (or her) every absurdity. What really goes on out on the course, and the golfer's life when not playing are chronicled in loving detail.

The Crazy World of the Handyman. £3.99. By Roland Fiddy. This book is a must for anyone who has ever hung *one* length of wallpaper upside down or drilled through an electric cable. A gift for anyone who has ever tried to "do it yourself" and failed!

The Crazy World of Hospitals. £3.99. By Bill Stott. Hilarious cartoons about life in hospital. A perfect present for a doctor or a nurse – or a patient who needs cheering up.

The Crazy World of Jogging. £3.99. By David Pye. An ideal present for all those who find themselves running early in the morning in the rain and wondering why they're there. They will find their reasons, their foibles and a lot of laughs in this book.

The Crazy World of Love. £3.99. By Roland Fiddy. This funny yet tender collection covers every aspect of love from its first joys to its dying embers. An ideal gift for lovers of all ages to share with each other.

The Crazy World of Marriage. £3.99. By Bill Stott. The battle of the sexes in close-up from the altar to the grave, in public and in private, in and out of bed. See your friends, your enemies (and possibly yourselves?) as never before!

The Crazy World of Music. £3.99. By Bill Stott. This upbeat collection will delight music-lovers of all ages. From Beethoven to Wagner and from star conductor to the humblest orchestra member, no-one escapes Bill Stott's penetrating pen.

The Crazy World of the Office. £3.99. By Bill Stott. Laugh your way through the office jungle with Bill Stott as he observes the idiosyncrasies of bosses, the deviousness of underlings and the goings-on at the Christmas party. ... A must for anyone who has ever worked in an office!

The Crazy World of Photography. £3.99. By Bill Stott. Everyone who owns a camera, be it a Box Brownie or the latest Pentax, will find something to laugh at in this superb collection. The absurdities of the camera freak will delight your whole family.

The Crazy World of Rugby. £3.99. By Bill Stott. From schoolboy to top international player, no-one who plays or watches rugby will escape Bill Stott's merciless exposé of their habits and absurdities. Over 80 hilarious cartoons – a must for all addicts.

The Crazy World of Sailing. £3.99. By Peter Rigby. The perfect present for anyone who has ever messed about in boats, gone pea-green in a storm or been stuck in the doldrums.

The Crazy World of Sex. £3.99. By David Pye. A light-hearted look at the absurdities and weaker moments of human passion – the turn-ons and the turn-offs. Very funny and in (reasonably) good taste.

The Crazy World of Skiing. £3.99. By Craig Peterson and Jerry Emerson. Covering almost every possible (and impossible) experience on the slopes, this is an ideal present for anyone who has ever strapped on skis – and instantly fallen over.

The Crazy World of Tennis. £3.99. By Peter Rigby. Would-be Pat Cashes and Chris Everts watch out.... This brilliant collection will pin-point their pretensions and poses. Whether you play yourself or only watch on TV, this will amuse and entertain you!

These books make super presents. Order them from your local bookseller or from Exley Publications Ltd, Dept BP, 16 Chalk Hill, Watford, Herts WD1 4BN. (Please send £1.50 to cover post and packing.)